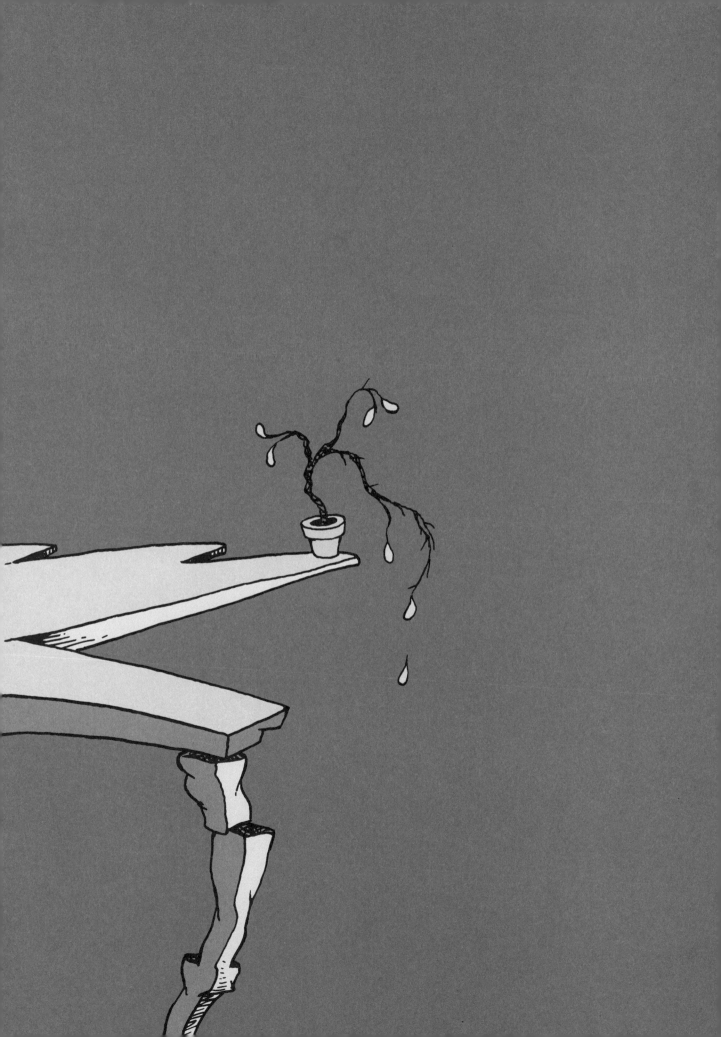

Did
I
Ever
Tell You
How Lucky
You Are ?

Did I Ever Tell You How Lucky You Are?

By Dr. Seuss

Random House • New York

Library of Congress Cataloging-in-Publication Data:
Seuss, Dr. Did I ever tell you how lucky you are?
SUMMARY: Compared to the problems of some of the creatures the old man describes, the boy is
really quite lucky.
[1. Fantasy.   2. Stories in rhyme]   I. Title.   PZ8.3.S477Di   [E]   73-5742
ISBN 0-394-82719-8; ISBN 0-394-92719-2 (lib. bdg.)

Manufactured in the United States of America   4 7

This Book,
With Love,
is for
Phyllis
the Jackson

When I was quite young
and quite small for my size,
I met an old man in the Desert of Drize.
And he sang me a song I will never forget.
At least, well, I haven't forgotten it yet.

He sat in a terribly prickly place.
But he sang with a sunny sweet smile on his face:

> When you think things are bad,
> when you feel sour and blue,
> when you start to get mad...
> you should do what *I* do!

Just tell yourself, Duckie,
you're really quite lucky!
Some people are much more…
oh, ever so much more…
oh, muchly much-much more
unlucky than you!

Be glad you don't work on the Bunglebung Bridge
that they're building across Boober Bay at Bumm Ridge.

It's a troublesome world. All the people who're in it
are troubled with troubles almost every minute.
You ought to be thankful, a whole heaping lot,
for the places and people you're lucky you're *not!*

Just suppose, for example,
you lived in Ga-Zayt
and got caught in that traffic
on Zayt Highway Eight!

Or suppose,
just for instance,
you lived in Ga-Zair
with your bedroom up here
and your bathroom up THERE!

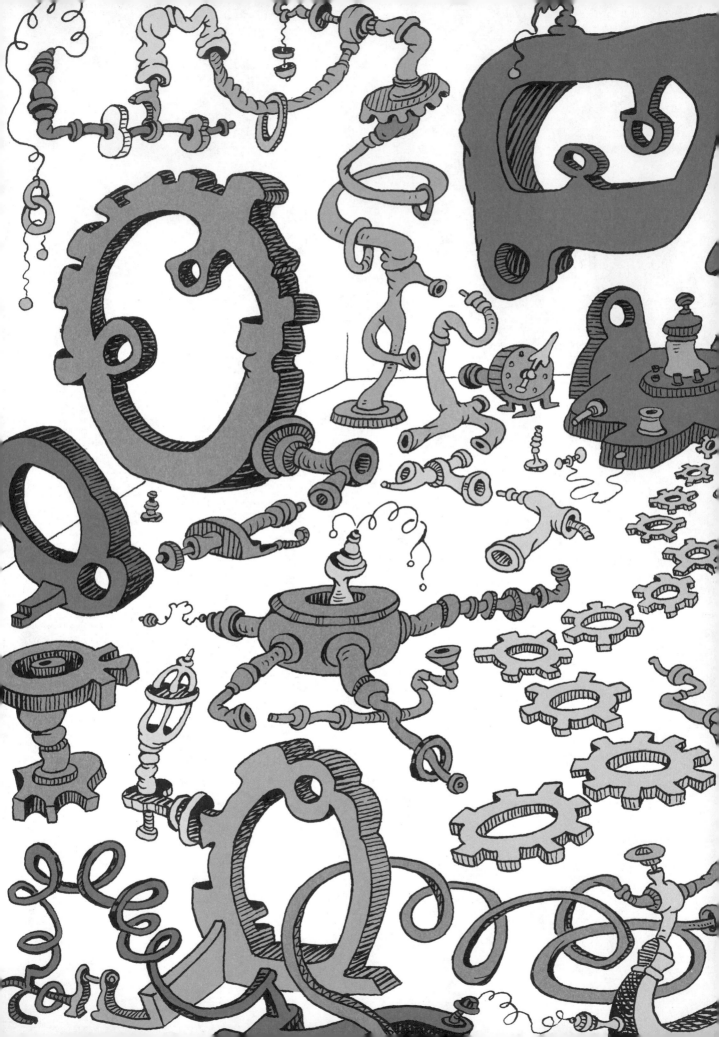

Suppose, just suppose, you were poor Herbie Hart,
who has taken his Throm-dim-bu-lator apart!
He *never* will get it together, I'm sure.
He never will know if the Gick or the Goor
fits into the Skrux or the Snux or the Snoor.
Yes, Duckie, you're lucky you're not Herbie Hart
who has taken his Throm-dim-bu-lator apart.

14

Think they work *you* too hard...?
Think of poor Ali Sard!
He has to mow grass in his uncle's back yard
and it's quick-growing grass
and it grows as he mows it.
The faster he mows it, the faster he grows it.
And all that his stingy old uncle will pay
for his shoving that mower around in that hay
is the piffulous pay of two Dooklas a day.
And Ali can't *live* on such piffulous pay!

                    SO...

He has to paint flagpoles
on Sundays in Grooz.
How lucky you are
you don't live in *his* shoes!

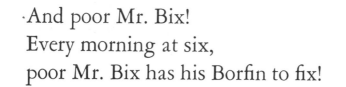

·And poor Mr. Bix!
Every morning at six,
poor Mr. Bix has his Borfin to fix!

It doesn't seem fair. It just doesn't seem right,
but his Borfin just seems to go shlump every night.
It shlumps in a heap, sadly needing repair.
Bix figures it's due to the local night air.

It takes him all day to *un*-shlump it.
And then...
the night air comes back
and it shlumps once again!

So don't *you* feel blue. Don't get down in the dumps.
You're lucky you don't have a Borfin that shlumps.

And, while we are at it, consider the Schlottz,
the Crumple-horn, Web-footed, Green-bearded Schlottz,
whose tail is entailed with un-solvable knots.

If *he* isn't muchly
more worse off than you,
I'll eat my umbrella.
That's just what I'll do.

And you're lucky, indeed, you don't ride on a camel.
To ride on a camel, you sit on a wamel.
A wamel, you know, is a sort of a saddle
held on by a button that's known as a faddle.
And, boy! If your old wamel-faddle gets loose,
I'm telling you, Duckie, you're gone like a goose.

And poor Mr. Potter,
        T-crosser,
        I-dotter.
He has to cross *t*'s
and he has to dot *i*'s
in an I-and-T factory
out in Van Nuys!

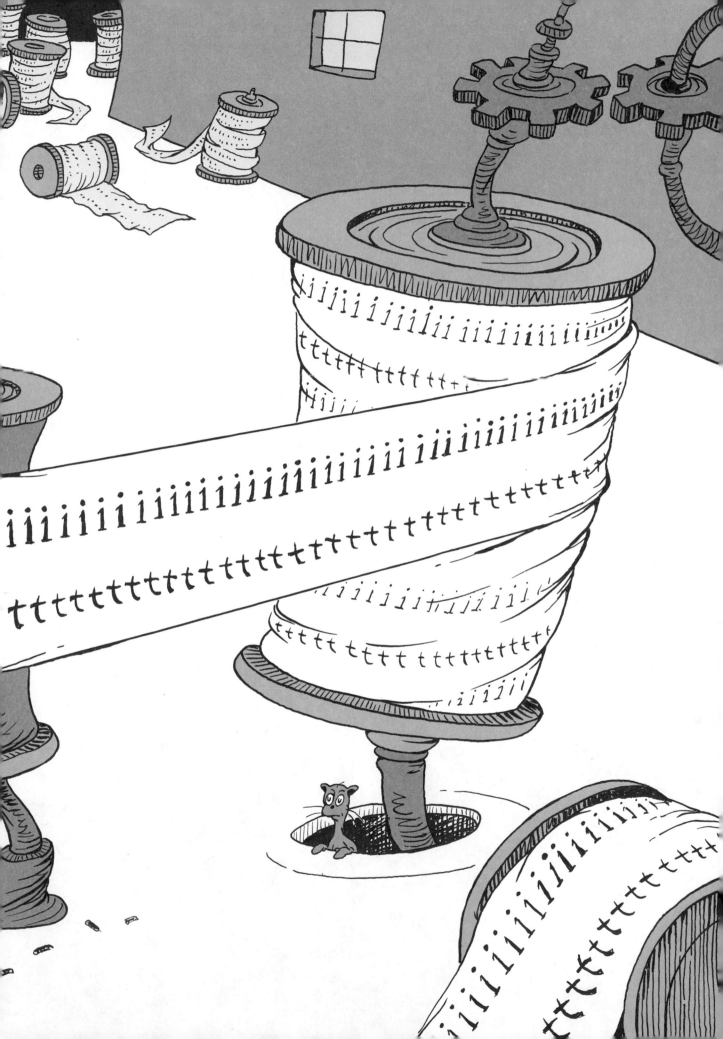

Oh, the jobs people work at!
Out west, near Hawtch-Hawtch,
there's a Hawtch-Hawtcher Bee-Watcher.
His job is to watch…
is to keep both his eyes on the lazy town bee.
A bee that is watched will work harder, you see.

Well…he watched and he watched.
But, in spite of his watch,
that bee didn't work any harder. Not mawtch.

So then somebody said,
"Our old bee-watching man
just isn't bee-watching as hard as he can.
He ought to be watched by *another* Hawtch-Hawtcher!
The thing that we need
is a Bee-Watcher-Watcher!"

WELL...

The Bee-Watcher-Watcher watched the Bee-Watcher.
He didn't watch well. So another Hawtch-Hawtcher
had to come in as a Watch-Watcher-Watcher!
And today all the Hawtchers who live in Hawtch-Hawtch
are watching on Watch-Watcher-Watchering-Watch,
Watch-Watching the Watcher who's watching that bee.
You're not a Hawtch-Watcher. You're lucky, you see!

And how fortunate *you're* not Professor de Breeze
who has spent the past thirty-two years, if you please,
trying to teach Irish ducks how to read Jivvanese.

And think of the
poor puffing Poogle-Horn Players,
who have to parade
down the Poogle-Horn Stairs
every morning to wake up
the Prince of Poo-Boken.
It's awful how often
their poogles get broken!

And, oh! Just suppose
you were poor Harry Haddow.
Try as he will
he can't make any shadow!

He thinks that, perhaps, something's wrong with his Gizz.
And I think that, by golly, there probably is.

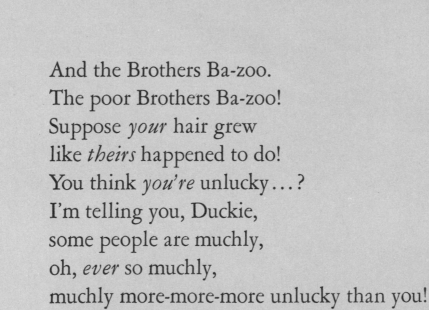

And the Brothers Ba-zoo.
The poor Brothers Ba-zoo!
Suppose *your* hair grew
like *theirs* happened to do!
You think *you're* unlucky...?
I'm telling you, Duckie,
some people are muchly,
oh, *ever* so muchly,
muchly more-more-more unlucky than you!

And suppose that you lived in that forest in France,
where the average young person just hasn't a chance
to escape from the perilous pants-eating-plants!
But *your* pants are safe! You're a fortunate guy.
And you ought to be shouting, "How lucky am I!"

And, speaking of plants,
you should be greatly glad-ish
you're not Farmer Falkenberg's
seventeenth radish.

And you're so, *so* lucky
you're not Gucky Gown,
who lives by himself
ninety miles out of town,
in the Ruins of Ronk.
Ronk is rather run-down.

And you're so, *so, So* lucky
you're not a left sock,
left behind by mistake
in the Kaverns of Krock!

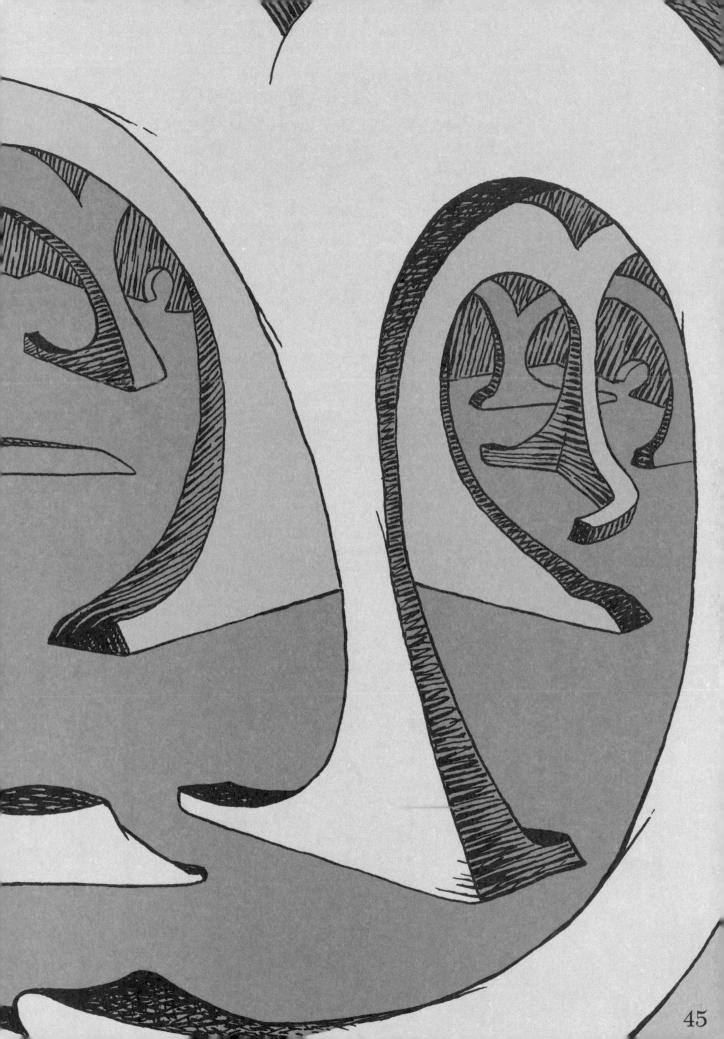

Thank goodness for all of the things you are not!
Thank goodness you're not something someone forgot,
and left all alone in some punkerish place
like a rusty tin coat hanger hanging in space.

That's why I say, "Duckie!
Don't grumble! Don't stew!
Some critters are much-much,
oh, ever so much-much,
so muchly much-much more unlucky than you!"

OTHER BOOKS BY DR. SEUSS

Yertle the Turtle and Other Stories
If I Ran the Circus
Horton Hears a Who!
Scrambled Eggs Super!
If I Ran the Zoo
Bartholomew and the Oobleck
Thidwick the Big-Hearted Moose
McElligot's Pool
Horton Hatches the Egg
And to Think That I Saw It on Mulberry Street
The 500 Hats of Bartholomew Cubbins
The King's Stilts
Happy Birthday to You!
How the Grinch Stole Christmas!
The Sneetches & Other Stories
Dr. Seuss's Sleep Book
I Had Trouble in Getting to Solla Sollew
The Cat in the Hat Song Book
I Can Lick 30 Tigers Today! And Other Stories
Did I Ever Tell You How Lucky You Are?
The Lorax
Hunches in Bunches
The Butter Battle Book
You're Only Old Once!
Oh, the Places You'll Go!

AND FOR BEGINNING READERS

The Cat in the Hat
The Cat in the Hat Comes Back
One Fish Two Fish Red Fish Blue Fish
Green Eggs and Ham
Hop on Pop
Dr. Seuss's ABC
Fox in Socks
The Foot Book
My Book About Me, by Me, Myself
Mr. Brown Can Moo! Can You?
I Can Draw It Myself, by Me, Myself
Marvin K. Mooney, Will You Please Go Now!
The Shape of Me and Other Stuff
Great Day for Up!
There's a Wocket in My Pocket!
Oh, the Thinks You Can Think!
I Can Read with My Eyes Shut
Oh Say Can You Say?
The Cat's Quizzer

Dr. Seuss